Decodes a Mystery

By Shannon Penney
Illustrated by Duendes del Sur

Hello Reader — Level 1

ISBN 0-439-67841-2

12 11 10 9 8 7 6 5 4   5 6 7 8 9 10/0

Designed by Louise Bova
Printed in the U.S.A.
First printing, February 2005

SCHOLASTIC INC.
New York   Toronto   London   Auckland   Sydney
Mexico City   New Delhi   Hong Kong   Buenos Aires

was at a birthday party.

All his friends were there.

They had .

They had .

They even had a piñata!

and wore blindfolds

and party .

They hit the piñata with a .

 broke the piñata.

 and went everywhere!

Now it was time to eat

lots of  !

 took off his blindfold.

He saw the .

He saw the 🎂 .

"Zoinks!" said . "The  is

all gone!"

"Ruh-roh," said .

"Like, maybe a 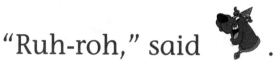 took the  !" said .

 hid under the .

looked for his friend.

He saw a on the floor.

Was the  a clue?

It was just a bunch of

and !

stuffed it in his .

They needed to find that !

"Maybe can help," said .

In the other room,  wore a blindfold.

He was playing pin the  on the .

"Can you help us find the , ?" asked .

But was busy.

He handed a , instead.

But the was just $142 \over 68$.

Maybe  could help!

 was outside, bobbing for

 in a  .

"Like, can you help us find the

 ,  ?" asked  .

But  had an  in her

mouth.

She couldn't speak.

She handed  another

instead.

"Rikes!" barked  .

This  was just more  !

Maybe could help.

They needed to find the

missing .

 was getting hungry!

The two friends found  playing musical 🪑.

" 🎩, the 🎺 is missing. Our only clues are, like, a bunch of **14²⁶⁸**!" said 😃.

"Maybe the 📄 that fell from the piñata will help," said 🎩, smiling.

"Zoinks! I think this is a code," said , looking at the ⬚ .

Each 14²6,8 matched a AD꜀ JFB .

When ⬚ and ⬚ decoded the other ⬚ , they read "HAPPY B-DAY!"

But they still didn't know who took the ⬚ .

Maybe it really *was* a ⬚ !

Just then, 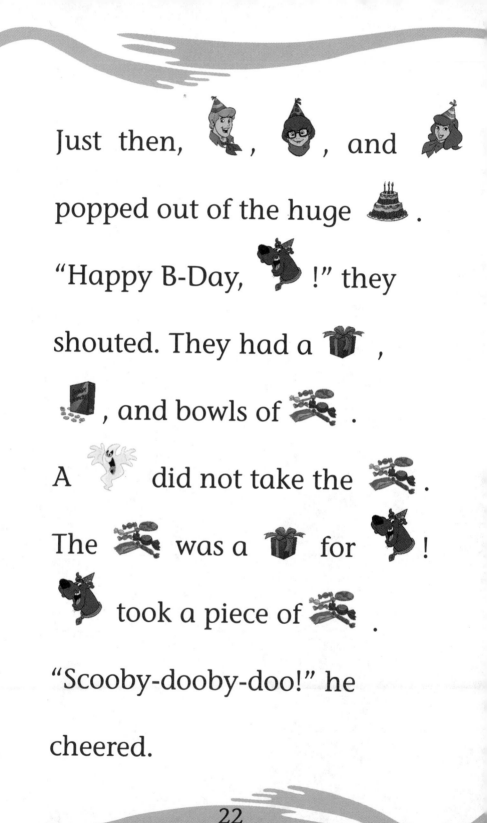, , and

popped out of the huge .

"Happy B-Day, !" they

shouted. They had a ,

, and bowls of .

A did not take the .

The was a for !

took a piece of .

"Scooby-dooby-doo!" he

cheered.

Did you spot all the picture clues in this Scooby-Doo mystery?

Each picture clue is on a flash card. Ask a grown-up to cut out the flash cards. Then try reading the words on the back of the cards. The pictures will be your clue.

Reading is fun with Scooby-Doo!

Shaggy	Scooby
Daphne	Fred
balloons	Velma

hats	cake
candy	stick
ghost	toys

note	table
tail	pocket
apples	donkey

chairs	bucket
numbers	gift
Scooby Snacks	letters